Ryan Respects

Virginia Kroll

illustrated by Paige Billin-Frye

ALBERT WHITMAN & COMPANY, MORTON GROVE, ILLINOIS

The Way I Act Books:

Forgiving a Friend • *Jason Takes Responsibility*

Honest Ashley • *Ryan Respects*

The Way I Feel Books:

When I Care about Others • *When I Feel Angry*

When I Feel Good about Myself • *When I Feel Jealous*

When I Feel Sad • *When I Feel Scared* • *When I Miss You*

Library of Congress Cataloging-in-Publication Data
is available from the Library of Congress.

Text copyright © 2006 by Virginia Kroll. Illustrations copyright © 2006 by Paige Billin-Frye.
Published in 2006 by Albert Whitman & Company,
6340 Oakton Street, Morton Grove, Illinois 60053-2723.

Printed in the United States of America.
10 9 8 7 6 5 4 3 2 1

The design is by Carol Gildar.

For more information about Albert Whitman & Company,
please visit our web site at www.albertwhitman.com.

For the McGowan children:
Patrick, William, and Jane.—V.K.

Every day Ryan walked to school with his friend Amy.

"Hey, Amy, what kind of bug is this?" he asked one day as he crouched on the sidewalk.

Amy bent down. "It's not a bug," she said. "It's actually a mollusk called a slug. It's a snail without a shell." Amy knew a lot about nature.

"Cool," said Ryan. "It's so slimy."

"It has to get under a rock where it's damp so it doesn't dry out before the sun gets any hotter," Amy said.

"Good thing there are rocks right near your porch," Ryan pointed out. "Because that slug sure is slow."

When Ryan and Amy got to school, they saw Doug. He looked nervous.

"What's wrong?" Ryan asked him.

"We're having a running test in gym today," Doug said. "I hope I'm fast enough."

"Well, I'm glad I'm as fast as a cheetah," Ryan said. Amy had told him the cheetah was the fastest animal.

That morning for Show and Tell, Joshua showed a
picture of himself in his Uncle Donald's airplane. Kimberlee
brought the fox she had molded out of clay. Ryan told about
the slug and the facts that Amy had taught him about it.

When gym class finally came, Ryan was ready. He ran like lightning. "You were a blur," said Amy. Everyone cheered for him.

Doug trailed behind them all.

After all the scores were timed, Ryan yelped,
"I'm the fastest. Told ya!"
Doug frowned. "And I'm the slowest."

Ryan thought of the creature from the sidewalk. "Right, Doug the Slug." He laughed, proud of his rhyme.

Doug's face burned red, and he looked like he might cry. But Ryan was too happy about his swift running time and too busy repeating the name to notice.

Some of his classmates laughed and joined in: "Doug the Slug!"

On the way home, Amy said, "You made Doug feel really bad. It wasn't nice, calling him a slug."

"Well, it's true, isn't it?" said Ryan.

"Maybe it is, but how would you feel if somebody did that to you?" Amy asked.

"They wouldn't. I'm the cheetah, remember?" Ryan bragged.

"You know what I mean," said Amy.

At bedtime, Dad tucked Ryan in and kissed him goodnight.
"Dad?" Ryan whispered, nodding toward the chair where he kept
his stuffed rabbit, Floppy.

"Oh," said Dad, "how could I forget?" He grabbed Floppy and snuggled him next to Ryan's cheek. Ryan caught a glimpse of his older brother, Judd, right outside the door just before Dad turned out the light.

Suddenly Judd popped in, sneering. "Cryin' Ryan, Cryin' Ryan, needs a teddy to go to beddy," he teased, reaching for Floppy.

"Floppy's a *rabbit*, Judd," said Ryan.

"Whatever. You're still Cryin' Ryan if you need him to sleep."

Ryan clutched Floppy tightly. He felt safer and slept better when Floppy was in bed with him. But when Judd said that, Ryan *did* feel like a scaredy-cat little baby. And what if Judd told Amy and the rest of Ryan's friends?

BLINK. The light flicked back on. "Stop that," Dad ordered. "I won't allow any name-calling. It's disrespectful and hurtful. And anyway, lots of kids even older than Ryan have bedtime friends like Floppy. I seem to remember another teddy in this house named Growler not so long ago," he said. Growler was Judd's old bear.

Dad went on. "And remember how you felt last year when your team lost the Word Wizards contest?" he asked Judd.

"Yeah," Judd recalled. "Anthony called me Judd the Dud because I missed a word. Some of the other kids called me that, too. I felt about as big as an ant."

Dad left the room but Judd stayed a moment longer. The look on his face and the tone in his voice had changed. He said, "Hey Ryan, I'm really sorry," and Ryan could tell that Judd really meant it.

As Ryan breathed deeply and relaxed, he thought of the slug and of his own rhyme that morning. He thought of what Amy and Dad had said about disrespect and hurt, and he knew that they were right. Now he also knew exactly how Doug had felt.

"I'll tell Doug 'sorry' first thing tomorrow," he whispered to Floppy. Then he hugged him tightly and fell fast asleep.